Cheryl
the Christmas
Tree Fairy

Special thanks to Rachel Elliot

To Emile and Isabella,
with love

ISBN 978-0-545-45571-8

12 11 10 9 8 7 6 5 4 3 2 1   12 13 14 15 16 17/0

Printed in the U.S.A.   40
First Scholastic printing, September 2012

Cheryl
the Christmas
Tree Fairy

by Daisy Meadows

SCHOLASTIC INC.

The Fairyland Palace

Fairyland Nursery

Fairy Homes

Seeing Pool

Christmas Cabin

Christmas future, Christmas past,
Let this festive magic last!
Steal away all Christmas joy
From every little girl and boy.

My Christmas will be full of glee
Thanks to the magic Christmas tree.
Those little fairies think they're clever
But I will stop their fun forever!

Ⓠ **Find the hidden letters in the ornaments throughout this book. Unscramble all 8 letters to spell a special Christmas word!**

Ⓐ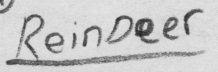

The Christmas Tree

Contents

Christmas Cabin

"Look at all the snow!" Kirsty Tate said happily.

She jumped into a powdery pile and squealed in delight.

"It's so beautiful," said her best friend, Rachel Walker. "I love it here already!"

"And you haven't even seen the inside of the cabin yet!" said her dad with a

laugh. "Come on, you two. You can decorate the Christmas tree."

"Oh, yes!" exclaimed Kirsty. "Each cabin comes with its own Christmas tree, doesn't it?"

Kirsty's and Rachel's parents had been planning this Christmas trip for months. They had booked a big cabin in the country for everyone to share. It was made of brown wooden logs that glowed in the winter sunshine, and a thick layer of snow covered the roof. There was a sign on the door that read: CHRISTMAS CABIN.

The Walkers and the Tates carried their bags into the cozy cabin. A fire was

2

crackling in a woodburning stove. Large squishy couches and armchairs filled the room, and colored Christmas lights were draped around every window. It was beautiful! There was just one problem. . . .

"Where's the tree?" asked Rachel.

Mr. and Mrs. Tate checked the kitchen, Mr. and Mrs. Walker checked the dining room, and Kirsty and Rachel checked the bedrooms. But there was no Christmas tree anywhere in the cabin.

"That must be a mistake," said Mr. Tate. "Let's go to the main office and clear

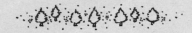

it up. I'm sure they'll have an extra tree for us!"

"Why don't you girls stay here and unpack your bags?" Mrs. Walker said to Rachel and Kirsty. "When we come back, we'll all have hot chocolate and marshmallows by the fire!"

Rachel and Kirsty agreed happily and raced into their bedroom to unpack. Rachel put all her clothes into the closet right away, but Kirsty was distracted.

"Look at the frost on the windows!" she said. "It looks just like lace."

Rachel joined her best friend beside the window. The tiny panes of glass were decorated with icy patterns.

"Everything's pretty here," she said, "even the ice!"

"I bet Jack Frost would love it," Kirsty said, smiling.

"He's the kind of frost we *don't* want this Christmas!" Rachel replied with a giggle.

Rachel and Kirsty knew they were very lucky—they were friends with all the fairies in Fairyland! Jack Frost and his naughty goblins were always trying to cause trouble, and Rachel and Kirsty had often helped the fairies stop them.

Kirsty turned to finish unpacking, but Rachel kept gazing out the window. Suddenly, she noticed something fluttering on the other side of the glass. The frost and snow made it difficult to see what it was. Rachel leaned closer until her nose was touching the cold windowpane. Were those . . . wings?

"Kirsty!" Rachel cried in excitement. "Come and look at this!"

Kirsty rushed to join Rachel at the window. Suddenly, there was a bright sizzle of golden light. It looked like someone had lit a sparkler outside!

Then the frost on the window melted away. The girls saw a beautiful fairy hovering outside, smiling and waving at them. It was Holly the Christmas Fairy!

Rachel opened the window and Holly fluttered inside. Her long dark hair was sparkling with snowflakes, and she was wearing a hooded red dress with fuzzy trim.

"Hello, Rachel!" she cried in her pretty, tinkly voice. "Hi, Kirsty! I'm so glad I found you."

"Holly!" said Rachel in delight. They'd had a wonderful Christmas adventure with Holly once. They had helped

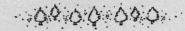

her save her Christmas magic from Jack
Frost and his goblins.

"It's so good to see you again," Kirsty
added. "But what are you doing in here?"

"I came to find you," said Holly. "I
really need your help! Will you come
with me to Fairyland—right now?"

"Of course!" said Rachel. "But what's happened?"

"I'll explain everything when we get there," Holly promised. "But we have to go now—the other winter fairies are waiting for us!"

Old Friends!

Holly flicked her wand and a stream of sparkling red fairy dust flew out of it. The fairy dust coiled around the girls like ribbons, and they began to shrink down to fairy-size. Beautiful sparkly wings appeared on their backs.

"I love having wings!" Rachel exclaimed, fluttering them in delight.

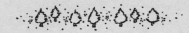

The berry-red sparkles swirled around them faster and faster, and the girls felt their feet lift off the ground. Holly took their hands as they spun through the air. When the sparkles faded, they found themselves in Fairyland! The grass was

hidden underneath a white carpet of snow, and fluffy snowflakes were falling from the sky. In the distance, the pink turrets

of the Fairyland Palace were glittering with snow, too.

"Welcome to the nursery," said Holly. "This is where we look after all the baby trees in Fairyland."

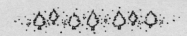

Rachel and Kirsty turned around and saw that they were standing in front of a group of pretty little trees. Best of all, hovering among the trees were their winter fairy friends!

"There's Gabriella!" cried Rachel, rushing over to hug the Snow Kingdom Fairy. "And Paige the Christmas Play Fairy!"

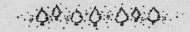

"I'm so glad to see you both again," said Stella the Star Fairy with a beaming smile.

"Thank you for coming," said Gabriella. "When Cheryl told us what had happened, we thought of you two right away."

"Who's Cheryl?" asked Kirsty.

A dark-haired fairy with a sad expression was standing in a circle of baby pine trees. She wore a red dress, a green shrug, and tall red boots trimmed with white fake fur. The neckline of her dress was decorated with a green bow, exactly the same color as a Christmas tree. She stepped forward and gave the girls a weak smile.

"Hello," she said. "I'm Cheryl the Christmas Tree Fairy. I look after the

Fairyland Christmas tree. When the tree
is decorated, celebrations can begin in
Fairyland and the human world. The
tree helps get everyone in the Christmas
spirit."

"That sounds like a really wonderful
job!" said Rachel, smiling back at the
little fairy.

"It is," said Cheryl. "I look forward to
it very much. I have two other magic

objects, too. The Christmas star helps everyone feel helpful and kind at Christmas, and the Christmas gift helps make sure that everyone enjoys the festivities, especially on Christmas day. But this year, everything's gone wrong!"

"Why?" asked Rachel. "What happened?"

"It all started this morning," said Cheryl. "You see, today is a really special day. I come here to the Fairyland Nursery on this day every year. I choose one of the young pine trees to be my special Christmas tree."

Her eyes filled up with tears, and the other fairies put their arms around her.

"Let's take Rachel and Kirsty to the Seeing Pool to show them what happened," said Holly.

The fairies led Rachel and Kirsty to the center of the nursery, where tiny green trees surrounded a glassy pool of water. Cheryl waved her wand over the pool, and the water shimmered with golden fairy dust as a picture formed. In the image, they could see Cheryl and the other winter fairies standing around a Christmas tree in the nursery.

"I chose the Christmas tree and all the other winter fairies joined me here for the

ceremony," said Cheryl. "You see, when I have chosen the tree, I say a magic spell. As soon as the spell is cast, everyone in Fairyland and the human world starts to feel happy and Christmasy."

Rachel and Kirsty stood beside Cheryl,

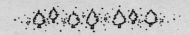

wondering just what had happened to upset her so much.

Kirsty looked at Rachel and frowned. "No one seems very Christmasy at all right now!" she whispered.

Jack Frost Attacks!

In the image, Cheryl waved her wand over the tree and it began to sparkle. Then she placed a shimmering purple and pink star on top of the tree.

"That's the Christmas star," Cheryl whispered to Rachel and Kirsty. "And look, that's the special Christmas gift."

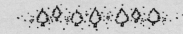

In the Seeing Pool, Rachel and Kirsty saw Cheryl put a present under the tree. It was wrapped in red paper with a Christmas-tree pattern and had a sprig of holly tied on top.

"I usually have to give a final wave of my wand to complete the Christmas magic," said Cheryl. "But before I could do that—look what happened!"

Rachel and Kirsty gazed into the pool. They saw Cheryl lift her arm to wave her wand. Then there was a big blue flash like a bolt of lightning! When the light cleared, the winter fairies were scattered around the nursery as if someone had knocked them down.

Worst of all, Jack Frost and three of his goblins were standing next to the Christmas tree! Jack Frost glared at the

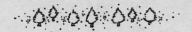

fairies and stroked his icy beard.

"You silly little fairies have had your silly little Christmas tree ceremony for the last time," he cackled. He grinned at the goblins. "Seize them!"

The goblin closest to the tree grabbed the Christmas star.

"No!" cried Cheryl, raising her wand.

But as she did, Jack Frost sent a lightning bolt that knocked the wand out of her hand.

"Not so fast, little fairy!" he jeered.

The second goblin picked up the special Christmas gift, and the third goblin reached around the magic Christmas tree and tried to lift it.

"OW!" he hollered as pine needles pricked his face and arms. "Ooh! Ouch!"

"Oh, stop complaining," snapped Jack Frost.

"Please stop!" cried Cheryl. "If you take these things away, Christmas will be ruined for everyone."

"Not for me," Jack Frost declared triumphantly. "And I'm the one that

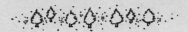

matters! I'm sick of having the same old Christmas as everyone else. This year, my Christmas is going to be the best in the whole world!"

"How can you enjoy it if it makes other people miserable?" asked Cheryl.

Jack Frost glared at her and then cackled. "That just makes it even better!" he declared.

"I won't let you get away with this," Cheryl said, putting her hands on her hips.

"You don't have a choice," Jack Frost snarled.

He waved his wand and all three goblins disappeared—along with the magical Christmas objects!

"No!" cried Cheryl.

"You'll never see your precious tree, star,

or gift again," Jack Frost declared. "You

pesky fairies think you're so great, but I'm too smart for you this time!" With a final cackle, Jack Frost waved his wand and disappeared.

The picture in the Seeing Pool faded, and Rachel and Kirsty turned to Cheryl.

"We won't ever let Jack Frost ruin Christmas," said Rachel in a determined voice.

"He's not as smart as he thinks he is," Kirsty added. "I bet we can figure out

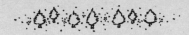

where he's hidden the tree, the star, *and* the gift."

"But there are only three days until Christmas," said Cheryl, looking worried. "There's not much time!"

Rachel and Kirsty put their arms around the little fairy and smiled.

"Then we'd better get started right away!" said Rachel.

Gloomy Goblins

Suddenly, Paige gave a loud gasp.

"The king and queen will wonder what happened," she said.

"You should all go and tell them what Jack Frost has done," said Cheryl.

"But we want to help you," said Stella.

"I have Rachel and Kirsty," said Cheryl, smiling at the girls. "The king and queen will need all of you to help with the other Christmas preparations."

The other winter fairies hugged them good-bye and wished them luck, and then they flew off to find the king and queen. Cheryl looked at the girls.

"I wish I felt as confident as you," she said. "But I have no idea where to start looking for my magic objects."

Rachel frowned. "I think we should

 start in the most obvious place," she said. "Maybe Jack Frost has taken everything to his Ice Castle."

Cheryl gave a little shiver. "It's a horrible place," she said. "Are you sure that you want to help me with this?"

"Of course!" Kirsty exclaimed bravely.

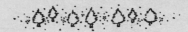

"Besides, we've been inside the Ice Castle before. We're not scared!"

"Then let's go!" said Cheryl.

They fluttered their wings and rose up into the air together. As they flew toward the Ice Castle, the air grew colder and dark clouds gathered overhead. They zoomed over a forest where the treetops were dusted with powdery snow.

"Look, Rachel," said Kirsty, pointing at the trees. "They look like cakes covered in powdered sugar!"

As Rachel looked down, she suddenly spotted something.

"What's that?" she asked, pointing and hovering in midair.

Kirsty and Cheryl peered down through the snowy trees. In a clearing, almost hidden from view, they could see three small green figures sitting in a circle. They were all pointing at one another with long, bony fingers. "Goblins," said Cheryl. "We must be pretty close to the Ice Castle."

"It looks like they're having an argument," said Kirsty thoughtfully.

"Goblins are so grouchy, they argue all

the time," Cheryl remarked. "Come on,
let's get to the castle."

"Just a minute," said Kirsty. "I have a
funny feeling about those goblins. Let's fly
a little lower and find out what they're up
to."

The three friends swooped silently
downward. They landed on a tree
branch above the goblins. Sure enough,
the goblins were in the middle of a big
argument.

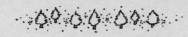

"It's not my fault!" a plump goblin was saying. "I thought *you* were watching it!" He jabbed his finger into the belly of a wart-covered goblin, who gave a yelp of pain.

"I was watching out for fairies!" he shrieked. "*He* was supposed to be guarding the tree!" He pointed at the smallest goblin, who was wearing a hat.

"Don't pick on me!" the smallest goblin exclaimed.

When the warty goblin mentioned the tree, the girls glanced at one another excitedly.

"Could it be *my* tree?" Cheryl whispered.

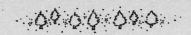

"Oh, I really hope so!" said Rachel.

"It must be," said Kirsty with confidence. "Why else would the goblins be guarding a tree?"

Down on the ground, the smallest goblin shoved the others to get their attention.

"Be quiet, you fools!" he said. "We need to figure out which one is the magic tree— before Jack Frost turns our noses into icicles."

When he said this, all three goblins clapped their hands over their noses and looked scared.

"We know it's somewhere in this forest,"

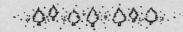

said the plump goblin. "Maybe we should just guard all the trees."

"Don't be crazy," snapped the warty goblin. "There are hundreds of trees in this forest, and there are only three of us!"

"Well, I don't hear you coming up with a better plan!" yelled the plump goblin, clenching his fists.

The two goblins hurled themselves

at each other and rolled around the
clearing, wrestling and yelling.

"Of course they can't find it," said
Cheryl in a low voice. "As soon as the
magic Christmas tree is taken out of the
nursery, it loses its sparkle. It looks like
an ordinary tree again!"

D

The Smell of Success!

"Can *you* tell which one is the magic Christmas tree?" Rachel asked Cheryl.

"I can cast a spell to make it sparkle again," said Cheryl, nodding.

"But first we have to get the goblins out of the clearing," Kirsty realized. "Cheryl, get your wand ready. I've got an idea!"

With that, Kirsty, Rachel, and Cheryl flew high above the treetops.

"We have to keep the goblins away from us," Kirsty said. "Cheryl, can you use your magic to make that happen?"

"Of course, but what will tempt them away?" said Cheryl.

The girls thought hard for a moment.

"I know!" said Rachel suddenly. "If you conjure up a wonderful food smell, I'm sure they'll try to find where it's coming from! We know how greedy goblins are."

Cheryl immediately flicked her wand, and a swirl of steam came out of it. The steam drifted down to the goblins. It smelled like pumpkin pies and chocolate brownies. It even made the girls feel hungry!

The goblins raised their noses into the

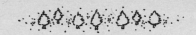

air as the steam drifted by.

"Food!" exclaimed the plump goblin, scrambling to his feet.

"That smells *so* good!" cried the warty goblin.

Cheryl sent the ribbon of steam off through the trees, and the three goblins followed it

eagerly. Then she whispered a few magic words and waved her wand. Silver glitter floated down and landed on the treetops. The girls scanned the area eagerly, but they didn't see a magical Christmas tree.

"It's not here," said Cheryl sadly.

"Let's try another area," Rachel suggested. They couldn't give up yet!

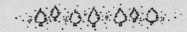

Cheryl used the delicious-smelling
steam to send the goblins even farther
away from them. Then she waved her
wand over a new group of trees. This
time, they saw something glittering far
below.

"Oh, please let it be my magic
Christmas tree!" Cheryl exclaimed.

They flew down into the forest. Among
a thick cluster of tall pines, they saw a
beautiful, sparkling Christmas tree.

"We found it!" squealed Rachel in
excitement.

Cheryl waved
her wand over the
tree, but nothing
happened.
"Oh, no! That
spell should

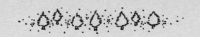

have sent the tree back to the Fairyland
Nursery!" cried Cheryl in alarm. "Jack
Frost must have put a sticking spell on it!"

"Can you break it?"
said Kirsty.

"Not by myself,"
Cheryl replied, looking
very upset.

"How can we help?" asked Rachel.

"I need to make the tree's magic
stronger than Jack Frost's spell," Cheryl
explained. "To do that we'll have to make
a circle around the tree and think hard
about how much we love Christmas. But
it really needs more than three people in
order to work. I don't know if we'll be
strong enough."

"Let's try!" said Kirsty, holding out her
hands.

They stood around the tree and held hands, making a circle. Then they closed their eyes and thought about Christmas as hard as they could. Rachel thought about Christmas treats and wrapping Christmas presents. Kirsty thought about singing carols and having fun with her family. They felt a rush of warmth passing through their hands.

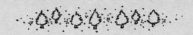

"That's it!" cried Cheryl, waving her wand again.

This time there was a loud *POOF!* The tree disappeared in a puff of red and gold fairy dust. Their plan had worked!

"Hooray!" said Cheryl. "Now let's deal with the goblins."

She drew the delicious-smelling steam back to her wand. A few seconds later, the girls heard the rustle of leaves and the snapping of twigs. Then the goblins pushed through the bushes in front of them.

"Fairies!" The goblin in the hat gasped.

"Did you greedy things eat all the food?" the

plump goblin asked suspiciously.

"No, but we already found the magic Christmas tree and sent it back to the Fairyland Nursery," said Kirsty, folding her arms.

The goblins groaned.

"We're in big trouble now!" wailed the warty one.

Cheryl waved her wand and a plate of mini pies appeared in front of the goblins.

"I'm sorry you're so cold and hungry," she said. "No one should be hungry at Christmastime, not even troublemakers!"

The goblins grabbed the plate of pies and gobbled them up as fast as they could. Cheryl hugged

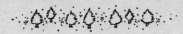

Rachel and Kirsty and gave them a beaming smile.

"Thank you," she said. "If it hadn't been for you, I never would have spotted the goblins in the forest."

"We're so glad we could help!" said Rachel.

"I'm going back to the palace to tell the king and queen that we found my magic Christmas tree," said Cheryl. "It's time for you two to go home. But I'll see you again soon!"

With that, Cheryl waved her wand. The girls were surrounded by a sparkly whirl of golden fairy dust. When it cleared, they were back at Christmas Cabin!

"Girls," called Mrs. Tate from the living room. "We got the tree!"

"There are some wonderful decorations here, too!" added Mrs. Walker. "And we just made some hot chocolate."

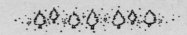

Rachel looked at Kirsty with shining eyes, and Kirsty gave a happy sigh.

"A tree to decorate, hot chocolate with marshmallows, and a fairy adventure," she said. "What a magical start to our Christmas vacation!"

The Christmas
Star

Contents

Santa's Village

The following morning, Rachel, Kirsty, and their parents were up bright and early. They had decided to take a sled-dog ride to a special place called Santa's Village.

"Are you looking forward to the ride, girls?" asked Mr. Walker.

Rachel and Kirsty nodded eagerly.

"I dreamed about sled dogs all night!" said Kirsty, laughing.

"I dreamed about Santa's Village," added Rachel. "There's a toy factory, a gift shop, and reindeer. The people who work there must be so nice!"

"Maybe they *won't* be nice if we can't find the magic Christmas star," Kirsty whispered to her friend in a worried voice. "The star is what helps everyone feel helpful and kind, remember?"

The girls knew that Jack Frost and his

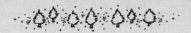

goblins had stolen three enchanted items from Cheryl the Christmas Tree Fairy. Kirsty and Rachel had helped her find the magical Christmas tree, but they still had to find the Christmas star and the Christmas gift—and time was running out. There were only two days left until Christmas!

"Let's go, girls!" said Mr. Tate.

Their sled guide was waiting for them outside. When the girls saw the husky dogs, they gasped in delight.

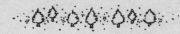

"They're so beautiful!" said Kirsty, her breath hovering in the chilly air.

Rachel and Kirsty loved the dogs' snow-tipped fur coats and bright, intelligent blue eyes. Everyone climbed into the sled and snuggled together under warm blankets.

"Mush!" cried the guide, and the huskies raced off.

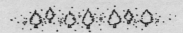

The dogs sped over the snowy ground, past pine trees, grazing reindeer, and cozy log cabins. The sled was going so fast that the cold wind took the girls' breath away, and no one could speak a word. But Kirsty and Rachel smiled at each other, their eyes sparkling.

The ride was over much too soon. The huskies slowed down as they arrived

in Santa's Village, and the sled stopped
outside a very large building. It was
decorated with colored lights and
had an arched sign over the door.

The girls and their parents jumped out
of the sled and made sure to say thank
you to the guide and the dogs. Then Mr.
Tate looked at his watch.

"Why don't you girls take a
look inside Santa's Workshop,
while we wander around
the gift shop?" he said.
"Then we can go for a
reindeer ride!"
Rachel and Kirsty nodded

and ran up to the door of Santa's Workshop. A man dressed as an elf opened the
door for them. He was wearing a bright-
green outfit with red trim.

"Welcome to Santa's Workshop," he said
with a beaming smile. "This is where we
make toys for children all over the world.
We're especially proud of the beautiful
wooden toys that our carpenters make."

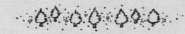

The girls stepped through the door and stopped in astonishment. The workshop seemed much, much bigger on the inside! Huge machines whirred all around them, letting out long whistles and shooting colored sparks into the air. Dozens of people dressed as elves rushed around busily.

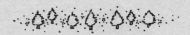

"Go ahead," said the man, who was
holding the door for them. "Just follow
the silver arrows painted on the floor.
You might even see Santa, if you're
lucky!"

Rachel and
Kirsty walked
on, following
the trail of
silver arrows
painted on the
workshop floor.

They came to a long table where
several carpenters were sitting in a row.
Each one was concentrating hard on the
toy he or she was making. Farther down
the line, more people dressed as elves were
painting wooden toys with bright colors.
Kirsty's eyes shined as she turned to her

best friend, but Rachel was frowning.

"What's wrong?" asked Kirsty.

Rachel pointed under the table, to where two very small elves were crouching. They were tying some of the carpenters' shoelaces together!

"Those naughty elves!" Kirsty exclaimed. She couldn't believe her eyes!

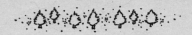

What were they thinking?

"Those aren't elves," said Rachel, as the troublemakers turned to each other, showing long green noses. "They're *goblins*!"

Cheryl to the Rescue!

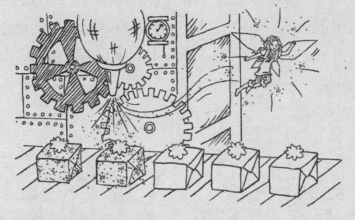

"Oh, no!" cried Kirsty. "What are they doing here?"

At that moment, a large machine beside them gave a loud whistle. Then there was a burst of red sparkles, and Cheryl popped out of the machine!

"Hello, girls!" she said.

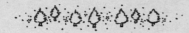

"Thank goodness you're here," said Rachel. "There are two goblins causing trouble over there!"

She quickly explained what had happened. When they turned back to the table, the goblins had disappeared—and all the carpenters' shoelaces were tied together!

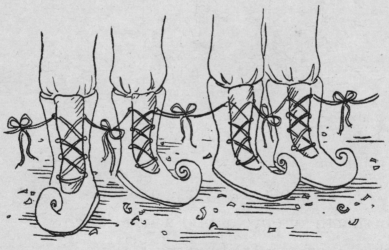

"I'd better fix that before someone gets hurt," said Cheryl, looking worried.

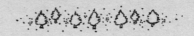

She waved her wand and said:

"Stop this silly goblin plot—
Untie each tangle and each knot!
Laces all should loop and show
On every foot a perfect bow."

The girls watched in awe as the shoelaces
untied themselves from one another and
formed neat bows.

"I can't
believe the
goblins are
here," said
Rachel.

"They're definitely
up to no good," Cheryl
said. "Let's follow them and find out what
they're doing!"

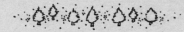

Cheryl tucked herself under a lock of Kirsty's hair so no one would see her. Then the girls followed the silver arrows deeper into the workshop, looking left and right for the goblins.

"Over there!" Kirsty exclaimed.

Two figures in green uniforms were kneeling down in front of a blue and red machine, peering into the engine. One of them was holding a wrench, and the other one had a hammer.

"We have to stop them," cried Rachel. "They're going to break the machine!"

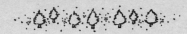

The girls dashed across and pulled
the figures away from the machine. But
to their horror, they saw two surprised
human faces staring at them!

"We're so sorry!" said
Kirsty, her cheeks
red with
embarrassment.
"We thought
you were . . .
someone else."

The girls
backed away
and rushed off
along the silver arrows'
path. As they walked farther into the
workshop, Cheryl gasped.

"I see them," she cried. "There they
are!"

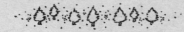

There was no doubt about it this time. The girls could see the goblins' green

faces! They were standing in a quiet corner next to a box full of toys, whispering to each other. "Come on," said Rachel. "Let's find out what they're saying."

The girls darted over to the other side of the box. They edged around it until they could hear the goblins' voices clearly.

"It's fun playing tricks on these silly people," the first goblin was saying. "What should we do next?"

"Playing tricks isn't the only reason we're here," said the second goblin. "Look

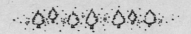

what I have."

He lifted his elf hat and the girls gasped.
Underneath the hat was something
purple and shiny.

"The Christmas star!" Cheryl gasped.

"What are you doing with that?" asked
the first goblin, his eyes almost popping
out of his head.

"Jack Frost is too mean to find a decent star for our tree," said the second goblin. "This one's terrible!"

"What's wrong with it?" asked the first goblin.

"It's too small," grumbled the second goblin. "I want an enormous star for our tree, and I'll bet there's a better one here. They make all sorts of pretty things in

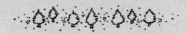

this place. I stole this star from Jack Frost so that we can swap it!"

"Oh my goodness," whispered Kirsty, her eyes wide. "The goblins don't know that the star has magical powers!"

Find Those Goblins!

The girls stared at one another in astonishment.

"How are we going to get the star back?" asked Cheryl.

"I've got a plan," said Rachel, her eyes shining. "The goblins are here to replace that star with something bigger. If we can find something they like, we might be able to convince them to trade!"

"I could make a star decoration that they'll love," said Cheryl, tapping her wand thoughtfully against her cheek. "It will have to be something big and colorful to please the goblins."

"Good idea," said Kirsty. "But first, we have to find them!"

She pointed to where the goblins had been standing. They had disappeared again!

"I wish they'd stop doing that," said Rachel. "Come on, let's go find them!"

The girls hurried through the workshop. They peered around machines, under tables, and inside crates of toys. They looked closely at all the workers they passed, and even checked the kitchen at

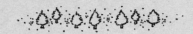

the back of the workshop. But there was
no sign of the goblins.

Suddenly, they heard someone yell,
"What do you think you're doing?"

The girls looked at each other in
excitement.

"I bet that's the goblins, causing
mischief!" Kirsty exclaimed. "Quick, let's
find out what's going on."

They ran over to where
the shout had come from.
A few people in elf
outfits were standing in
a huddle, hands on their
hips. Above their heads hung a sign that
read: TESTING AREA. Each of them was
wearing a badge that said: TOY TESTER.
Rachel and Kirsty peeked over their
shoulders.

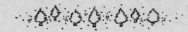

One of the goblins was sitting on a
wooden tricycle that was much too small
for him. He was pedaling around in
circles. There was a long piece of string
attached to the back of the tricycle,
which had wooden dolls, wooden blocks,
and a toy train tied to it. The toys were
crashing and bouncing along behind the
tricycle, and the goblin giggled as he
pedaled faster and faster.

"Stop!" cried the toy testers. "You're
breaking the toys!"

The second goblin was waving a bat around in one hand and throwing tennis balls into the air with the other. None of the elves could get near him.

"Wheeee!" he shouted.

He whacked a tennis ball with the bat. It soared into the air, hit the ceiling, and bounced off the head of one of the toy testers.

"Ouch!" he cried, rubbing his head.

"We have to stop them!" Rachel exclaimed.

She rushed forward and stepped on the string that was trailing from the back of the tricycle. She dug her heel into the ground. The goblin gave a yelp of anger and toppled off as the tricycle screeched to a stop.

"You horrible girl!" he squealed, leaping to his feet and hopping up and down in a fury. "You ruined my fun!"

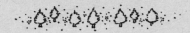

"We just want to talk to you—"
Rachel began.

But the goblin darted behind a table
piled high with toys and disappeared.
Meanwhile, Kirsty had run toward the
other goblin.

"Stop hitting those tennis balls," she
pleaded. "You'll hurt someone!"

The goblin stuck out his tongue and
made a face. Then he threw down the bat
and raced after his companion.

Goblins in Danger!

While the workers began to clean up the mess, Rachel and Kirsty headed off after the goblins. Cheryl was still hiding under Kirsty's hair so she wouldn't be spotted. Ahead, they saw three girls in elf outfits standing together. Each of them was holding a clipboard, and they all looked

very upset. "Is everything OK?" asked Kirsty, hurrying up to them.

"Someone ruined our checklists," said one of the girls. "We have to check to make sure that all the toys are safe to go into the gift shop. We mark off little boxes when we've checked that the toys work and are made well. But someone has put marks in *all* of the boxes on our sheets. We can't tell which are real and which aren't, so we'll have to start from scratch!"

"That's so mean," said Rachel.

"That sounds like the work of goblins," muttered Kirsty under her breath.

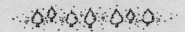

Suddenly, Rachel caught a glimpse
of a green foot as it disappeared around
a corner.

"What's over there?" she asked the elves,
pointing.

"Just the Reindeer Barn," the girl
replied.

Kirsty and
Rachel
exchanged a
worried
glance.

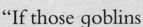

"If those goblins
upset the reindeer, no one will be able
to go for a sleigh ride today," Kirsty
whispered. "We have to stop them."

The girls ran over to where they had
seen the goblins and found a large
wooden door. The sign on the door said:

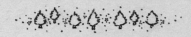

REINDEER BARN.

PLEASE KEEP THIS DOOR SHUT.

(AND NO EXTRA CARROTS FOR RUDOLPH.

HE'S ON A DIET.)

The door was swinging open.

"Oh, no," said Rachel. "I think we're too late."

They stepped cautiously into the barn. The floor was covered with straw, and the barn was lined with empty stalls. Each stall had a different name printed on it.

"Dancer . . . Prancer . . . Vixen . . ." Kirsty read aloud. "This is where the reindeer live—but where are they now?"

"They're out on a sleigh ride," said a voice behind them.

The girls whirled around and saw the man who had let them into the workshop.

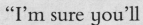

"I'm sure you'll see them another time," he said. "But this door is supposed to be kept closed."

The girls smiled at him, apologized, and went back into the workshop.

"That's a relief," said Rachel. "The barn must have been empty when the goblins got there."

"But where did they go next?" asked Kirsty.

"I think I know!" said Cheryl, flying

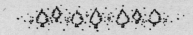

out from under Kirsty's hair. "Look at that."

She pointed at the floor. There were a few strands of straw leading away from the barn door.

"Ooh, let's follow them," said Rachel. Cheryl fluttered ahead of the girls as they followed the trail of straw. While they hurried along, they heard a hum of chatter that grew louder and louder. The straw trail ran out, but by then they could follow the sound of the voices.

They turned a corner and saw another group of angry-looking people staring at a big red and gold machine. The

goblins were dancing on the edge of the machine!

"Come down here now!" the head carpenter demanded. But the goblins kept jumping around, sticking their tongues out at the workers surrounding them.

Suddenly, one of the goblins wobbled, shrieked, and clutched at the other. They both lost their balance—and tumbled into the machine!

Goblin Gifts

The machine let out a series of whistles and beeps. There were even some loud clunks.

"Oh, no!" cried Rachel. "We have to rescue them!"

"What kind of machine is that?" Kirsty asked the head carpenter.

"It's an automatic wrapping machine,"

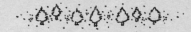

he replied. "It can wrap any present,
any size."

"Will they be all right?" asked Rachel.

"They'll be fine," said the head
carpenter, looking angry. "Just a little
shocked. Maybe it will teach them
a lesson!"

A large chute opened at the base of the
machine, and two goblin-shaped presents

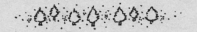

popped out. They were wrapped in shiny Christmas paper!

Rachel and Kirsty hurried over and tore the paper at the end of each present. Angry green goblin faces appeared.

"Let us go!" they demanded, struggling in the wrapping. "It's not funny!"

"It *is* pretty funny," said Rachel, stifling a giggle.

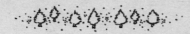

"We're not letting you go until you've listened to what we have to say," said Kirsty as the elves all wandered off.

The goblins grumbled and wriggled, but they couldn't get away. Rachel and Kirsty kneeled down in front of them, and Cheryl fluttered onto Rachel's knee.

"I should have known," muttered the first goblin when he saw her. "Pesky fairies!"

"Listen," said Rachel. "We want to help you. We overheard you saying that you want a bigger decoration for the top of your tree. Cheryl will make one for you, if you'll swap your star for it."

The goblins narrowed their eyes suspiciously.

"Why would you do that?" asked the second goblin.

"Because we like your star," said Kirsty truthfully. "And it's Christmas. People are supposed to be extra nice to one another at Christmastime."

"I could make you the very best tree decoration you've ever seen," said Cheryl.

The goblins looked at each other and nodded.

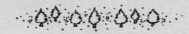

"All right," they said. "Show us!"

Rachel and Kirsty tore away the rest of the wrapping paper, while Cheryl waved her wand. Golden fairy dust streamed from the tip of her wand and zigzagged into the shape of a large gold star. Red, blue, and yellow jewels sparkled in the center. It hung in the air in front of the goblins, and their mouths fell open in wonder.

"Well?" asked Rachel, holding her breath.

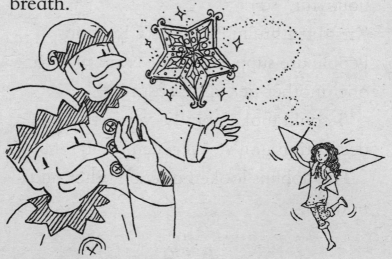

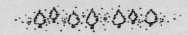

"It's the most beautiful decoration I've ever seen!" cried the first goblin.

The second goblin lifted his hat, took out the magic Christmas star, and handed it to Cheryl. She waved her wand again and returned the Christmas star to its fairy size.

"I don't know how to thank you girls," she said, smiling at Rachel and Kirsty.

"Just return the star to the magic Christmas tree," said Kirsty. "Then everyone will start feeling helpful and kind!"

"And that's what Christmas is all about," Cheryl said.

She blew them a kiss and disappeared in a flurry of fairy dust.

Moments later, the girls felt a warm glow all around them. It gave them a  wonderful happy feeling. They just wanted to smile at everyone! "That must mean that the magic Christmas star is back where it belongs," said Rachel.

Nearby, the first goblin tucked the huge star under his arm and rubbed his hands together.

"Time to get back to the Ice Castle," he said.

"Wait a minute," said the second goblin. "Maybe we should stay here and help the elves clean up."

"Oh," the first goblin said. "You're right.

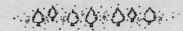

We did make an awfully big mess."
Rachel and Kirsty watched in
amazement as the goblins hurried off
to help the elves.

"Well," said Kirsty, finding her voice at
last, "I guess the magic Christmas star
must have affected the goblins, too."
"And that's what I call powerful
magic!" Rachel said, giggling.

The Christmas Gift

Contents

News from Fairyland

"Could you pass me the gold ribbon, please?" Rachel asked Kirsty. "I want to make Mom's present look extra special."

It was Christmas Eve, and the girls were busy wrapping presents in their room at Christmas Cabin. It was dark, but they hadn't closed the curtains yet. Christmas lights twinkled in the window, and

snowflakes were falling outside.

"Christmas here is almost as magical as Fairyland," said Kirsty, handing the gold ribbon to her best friend and staring out the window.

"I hope that Christmas *will* be magical," Rachel said, tying the ribbon around the little box of perfume. "It will be ruined here *and* in Fairyland if we can't find Cheryl's magic Christmas gift." The girls and their families were on a Christmas vacation in the country, but as soon as they arrived, Jack Frost and his goblins had started causing trouble. They had taken Cheryl the Christmas Tree Fairy's special magical items!

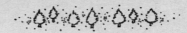

With Kirsty and Rachel's help, Cheryl
had found the Christmas tree and the
beautiful Christmas star—but the magic
Christmas gift was still missing.

"The Christmas gift helps make
sure that everyone enjoys the holiday
festivities," Kirsty remembered. "Oh,
Rachel, I hope Jack Frost doesn't ruin
Christmas day—or the midnight
caroling concert!"

"Me, too," said Rachel, wrapping up
her dad's present, which was a new bike
helmet. "It'll be so much fun!"

Rachel and Kirsty were very excited about Christmas day and the outdoor concert that evening. There were going to be carols, and the girls would be allowed to stay up late to sing!

"Somehow we have to find that magic Christmas gift, no matter what!" said Rachel, determined.

Suddenly, Kirsty gasped and pointed at the silver wrapping paper that Rachel was using. Golden sparkles were dancing around the edges of the paper.

"Those are fairy sparkles!" Kirsty exclaimed.

"You're right!" cried Rachel, letting

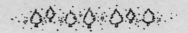

go of the paper.

The girls watched in delight as the paper wrapped itself around the bike-helmet box. Silvery ribbons curled around it and tied themselves into beautiful bows.

Then there was a puff of golden fairy dust, and Cheryl appeared in the midst of it! She flew into the air, until she was hovering face-to-face with the girls.

"Hi, girls," she said quietly. "I know where the magic Christmas gift is."

"That's wonderful!" said Rachel, clapping her hands together in excitement.

"So, where is it?" asked Kirsty eagerly.

Both girls thought it was strange that Cheryl didn't seem happy about the news. Her eyes looked worried, and she wasn't smiling.

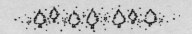

"I've been searching high and low in Fairyland," she said. "Everyone has joined in—even the king and queen. We've looked under every toadstool and investigated every bird's nest. No one has been able to find the magic Christmas gift."

"Does that mean it's here in the human world?" asked Rachel.

Cheryl shook her head. "I would know if it had left Fairyland because of my strong connection with it," she said. "This morning we finished our search, and Queen Titania said that there is only one place it could be . . . the Ice Castle."

Rachel and Kirsty exchanged worried looks. They had been in Jack Frost's chilling castle before, and it was cold and dangerous.

"Will you help me again, girls?" asked Cheryl, clasping her hands together. "I know it's a big favor, but I can't do it without you. Will you come and search

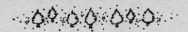

the Ice Castle with me?"

Rachel and Kirsty didn't hesitate. There was only one answer they could give.

"Yes!" they said together.

A Snowy Disguise!

Cheryl waved her wand, and a burst of golden fairy dust exploded from it like a tiny firework. It coiled around the girls' ankles and spiraled up around their bodies until they were glimmering with gold sparkles. Delicate wings sprouted from their backs as they shrank to fairy-size.

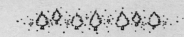

The golden sparkles became whirling
hoops of light, spinning around them.
Their bedroom vanished in a blur, and
when the light disappeared, the girls
found themselves standing in the forest
outside Jack Frost's
Ice Castle.
"Wow!" said
Kirsty. "I
think that
was the
fastest trip to
Fairyland ever!"
"We have to
be quick," said Cheryl in
an urgent whisper. "There are only a few
hours of Christmas Eve left. If midnight
strikes before I have the magic Christmas
gift back, it will be too late—and no one

will enjoy Christmas day!"

"But how are we going to get inside the castle?" asked Rachel. "There are bound to be guards on duty, and they won't let us just fly in."

Kirsty looked up into the darkening sky. Snowflakes were drifting down.

"I have an idea!" she said, her eyes sparkling. "Cheryl, could you disguise us as snowflakes? Then we could fly right into the central courtyard, and the goblin guards wouldn't suspect a thing!"

"That's a great idea!" said Cheryl.

The three friends zipped up into the sky

and hovered above the snowy courtyard
in the center of the castle. Sure enough,
there were several goblin guards on
duty. They were marching back and
forth across the courtyard, looking very
important.

Cheryl tapped Rachel and Kirsty with
her wand, and then touched it against her
own head. Instantly, they all shrank to
the size of snowflakes. They were coated

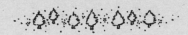

in white from head to toe, with sparkly
crowns on their heads!

"We look like
someone's
wrapped us
in white lace!"
Rachel giggled.

The girls flew
downward, making
sure that they moved
at the same speed as
the snowflakes around them.
Rachel couldn't help remembering the
time they had visited the castle with Belle
the Birthday Fairy. She shivered but tried
to stay brave.

"Head toward that hallway," she
whispered, pointing at a dark archway
in the courtyard wall. "That leads to the

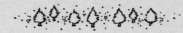

Great Hall—we can start our search there."

They landed under the archway. The goblin guards were still marching around the courtyard. They were wearing colorful hats and scarves to protect them from the cold.

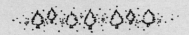

"Come on, before they notice us!"
whispered Cheryl, her breath hanging
in the icy air.

As the three friends
fluttered into the
corridor, their
snowflake
disguises
melted away
and they
returned to
fairy-size.
They flew quickly
to the Great Hall,
but the doors were wide
open—and it was empty.

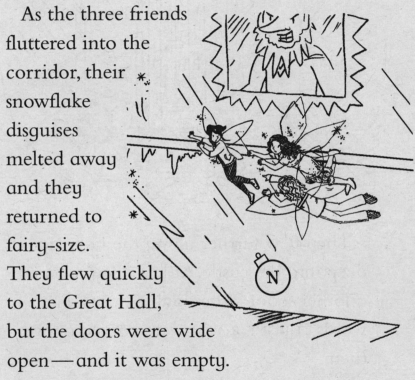

"We have to keep looking," Kirsty
whispered.

They flew farther along the hallway,
deep into the castle. At last, they reached
another set of large double doors. The
words THRONE ROOM were carved above
them.

"Listen!" said Rachel, putting her ear
to the door.

Someone was speaking in low, grumbling tones.

"I'd know that voice anywhere!" Rachel said.

Kirsty nodded firmly. "It's Jack Frost!"

Jack Frost's Mistake

Cheryl tapped her wand on the door and it slowly creaked open. The girls peered around it.

"There he is!" Cheryl gasped.

Jack Frost was sitting with one leg hooked over the arm of the throne and his spiky chin resting on his hand. He was staring at a small, sad-looking Christmas tree. Its only decorations were some big icicles and the huge star that Cheryl had made for the goblins.

"That poor little Christmas tree is so unloved," said Cheryl with a sigh.

"But look what's underneath it!" Rachel whispered in excitement.

Under the drooping branches of the tree was the magic Christmas gift!

"Those silly goblins have ruined my Christmas *again*," Jack Frost was muttering to himself. "Can't they do anything right? They lost the magic Christmas tree, gave away the magic Christmas star, and now they've 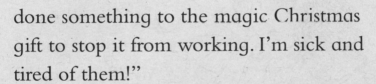 done something to the magic Christmas gift to stop it from working. I'm sick and tired of them!"

"What is he talking about?" asked Kirsty in a low voice. "The magic Christmas gift looks OK to me."

"I don't know," said Cheryl, lifting her chin bravely, "but I'm going to find out."

Before the girls knew it, Cheryl fluttered

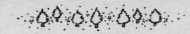

into the middle of the Throne Room.
Rachel and Kirsty took deep breaths and
flew close behind her. Jack Frost was still
staring at the tree, his eyebrows knitted
together in an icy frown. He hadn't
spotted them.

"Jack Frost!" said Cheryl loudly.

Jack Frost's head whipped around to

face them, and
his eyes widened
when he saw
the three fairies.
"You!" he snarled.
"How did you
get into my castle?"
"We're here to ask
you to return the magic
Christmas gift," said Rachel bravely.

"It's no use to you," Kirsty added.

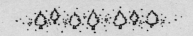

"Tell me how to make it work!"
Jack Frost roared, leaping to his feet.

Cheryl looked at
the girls in
confusion, and
Jack Frost gave
a howl of
rage.

"No fairy
tricks!" he shouted.

He pointed his wand
and a stream of ice bolts came hurtling
toward them!

"Duck!" cried Cheryl.

The three girls scattered, and the ice
bolts just missed them.

"Make it work, or I'll turn you all
into tiny ice sculptures and use you
as ornaments!" Jack Frost snarled.

"The magic Christmas gift can only do its job when it's in the Fairyland Nursery, underneath the magic Christmas tree," Cheryl explained, looking confused.

"You're lying!" Jack Frost hissed. "You just want to keep all the presents for yourself!"

"Fairies don't lie," said Cheryl indignantly. "I don't know what you're talking about. The magic Christmas gift doesn't bring presents."

Jack Frost sat down on his throne with a heavy thump, and his mouth fell open.

"What?" he said in disbelief.

"I think I understand what happened," said Rachel. "Jack Frost thought that the

magic Christmas gift would bring him
lots of presents — that's why he wanted
it."

Cheryl fluttered closer to the throne.

"That's not what the magic Christmas
gift does," she said gently. "You made
a mistake. Its job is to make sure that
everyone has a happy time on
Christmas day."

"Then it should give me hundreds of presents!" Jack Frost shouted.

"Presents can't make you happy," said Cheryl. "It's the magic and warmth of Christmas that does that."

Rachel and Kirsty fluttered closer.

"Please give back the magic Christmas gift," said Kirsty. "Then everyone can have a merry Christmas."

Jack Frost looked suspicious.

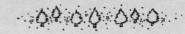

"Even me?" he asked.

"Yes," said Cheryl. "I promise that if you give me the magic Christmas gift, you'll have the jolliest Christmas you've ever had."

The girls held their breath. Would Jack Frost agree? He raised his wand and Rachel clutched Kirsty's arm. What was he going to do?

A Magical Invitation

Muttering a spell, Jack Frost pointed his wand at the magic Christmas gift.

It rose into the air and floated toward Cheryl, shrinking as it moved. By the time it landed in her arms, it was back to fairy-size. Jack Frost lowered his wand.

"Thank you!" said Cheryl, beaming. "I'll return the magic Christmas gift to its rightful place under the magic Christmas tree. Then you will see how wonderful Christmas can be!"

"All right," Jack Frost growled. "But just in case you're lying to me, those other two

can stay here until you get back." He pointed at Kirsty and Rachel. "That's not fair!" Cheryl gasped. "I told you, I'm not lying!"

"It's OK," said Rachel. "We'll wait for you here."

"Aren't you scared?" asked Cheryl in a low voice.

"Not when we're together," said Kirsty, linking arms with her best friend.

"I think you're both very brave," said Cheryl, blowing them a kiss.

She disappeared in a flash of golden sparkles, and Jack Frost glowered at Rachel and Kirsty.

"If she doesn't come back, I'm going to lock you both in my deepest dungeon," he said.

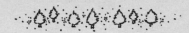

Rachel glanced at the tall windows
and shivered. It was dark outside, but the
moon's rays were shining on the swirling
snowflakes. Then she saw something
coming toward the window, flying
quickly through the snow.

"Kirsty, look!" she exclaimed.
The object got closer and closer,
curving down through the sky.

"It's going to crash through the window!" Kirsty cried.

Jack Frost dove behind his throne and the girls covered their faces, expecting to hear shattering glass. But all they heard was the tinkling of countless bells! They opened their eyes. Jack Frost was cowering behind his throne, but Kirsty and Rachel clapped their hands happily.

Standing in the middle of the Throne Room, draped in red velvet and tiny

silver bells, was Santa's sleigh! Nine
reindeer were stomping their hooves on
the stones and shaking the snow off their
furry coats.

"Hello, Jack Frost!" said one of the
reindeer in a gruff, dignified voice.

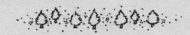

Jack Frost stepped out from behind his throne, adjusting his robes and clearing his throat.

"What do you want?" he demanded rudely.

"Santa sent us," said the reindeer. "He

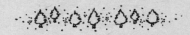

wants to thank you for returning the
magic Christmas gift to its rightful place.
He would like to invite you to help him
deliver the presents this year."

Jack Frost paused for a minute, his hand
resting on his icy chin. Then he let out a
little whoop of excitement and danced
around his throne, grinning.

"I've never seen him look so happy!"
said Rachel with a giggle.

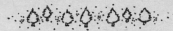

"Santa sends his greetings to you, too, Kirsty and Rachel," said the reindeer. "He knows what a great help you have been to the fairies."

Before they could reply, Rachel and Kirsty heard a whooshing sound above them. Golden fairy dust began to rain down from the ceiling. The girls gasped in delight. Everywhere the fairy dust touched was transformed before their eyes!

Silver and gold decorations hung from the ceiling, candles flickered in the windows, and sprigs of holly were pinned

to the walls. Best of all, the sad-looking
Christmas tree became tall and bushy,
draped with tinsel and sparkling with
ornaments. The big star glistened at
the top.

Cheryl the Christmas Tree Fairy was

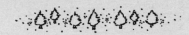

hovering in the middle of it all, smiling
with her wand held high.

"Merry Christmas, everyone!" she
exclaimed.

The Perfect Christmas

The Throne Room doors burst open and a crowd of goblins scampered in, wearing party hats and waving festive Christmas decorations. Each goblin seemed to be singing a different carol, and every one of them was out of tune.

Cheryl waved her wand, and a long
table appeared at the far end of the
Throne Room. It was covered with
platters of turkey and bowls of stuffing
and gravy, as well as Christmas cookies
and other yummy desserts.

"Party time!" the goblins squealed in
delight.

They dove in enthusiastically, pulling

Christmas snappers, telling jokes, and
gobbling down the delicious treats.
Meanwhile, Jack Frost had leaped into
the sleigh.

"Santa's house, here I come!" he
whooped.

The reindeer shook their antlers and the
sleigh rose into the air, turning toward the
window. Then there was a bright flash,

and in the blink of an eye, the reindeer
and the sleigh were on the other side of

the window,
galloping away into
the night.
Cheryl fluttered
down to the
girls.
"You did it!"
cried Kirsty
happily.
"*We* did it,"
Cheryl corrected
her. "Without your
help, I never could have gotten all of my
magical objects back in time."

"The goblins are warm and happy, and
Jack Frost is having his best Christmas
ever," said Rachel. "It's perfect!"

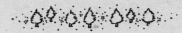

"*Almost* perfect," Cheryl said with a wink. "I still have to get you both home before midnight strikes!"

She threw her arms around them and hugged them tightly.

"You saved Christmas," she said. "I can't thank you enough. But I can make sure that you have a wonderful, merry Christmas!"

"Merry Christmas!" said Kirsty and Rachel, hugging her back.

A fountain of golden fairy dust burst
from Cheryl's wand and showered down
on the girls. They were dazzled by the
sparkles, and when their vision cleared,
they were back in their cozy room in
Christmas Cabin.
The presents
Rachel hadn't
finished
wrapping
earlier were
now
beautifully
wrapped
and labeled.
"Cheryl must
have done
that," said Kirsty
as they changed into their pajamas.

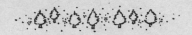

"That was nice of her!"

"Hasn't it been a wonderful Christmas adventure?" said Rachel, leaning over to close the curtains. "And I'm so excited about Christmas day — Oh! Kirsty, look!"

Kirsty dashed over to the window as Rachel flung it open. Santa's sleigh was silhouetted against the full moon!

The girls breathed in the crisp night air as they gazed up, their heads pressed close together. They could see the outline of a huge pile of presents in the back of the sleigh. A big man with a bushy beard and a red and white hat held the reins, and beside him they could see a thin, spiky figure.

As the sleigh disappeared into the distance, they heard a voice ringing in the night air.

"Ho, ho, ho!"

"That's Jack Frost!" said Rachel in delight.

The best friends looked at each other and smiled.

"Come on, let's go to bed and wait for Santa to visit *us,*" said Kirsty. "I think everyone will have a very merry Christmas after all!"

SPECIAL EDITION

Don't miss any of Rachel and Kirsty's other fairy adventures. Check out this magical sneak peek of

Florence
the Friendship Fairy!

Magic Memories

Rachel Walker pulled a large scrapbook from underneath Kirsty Tate's bed, and the two best friends opened it between them. It was their memory book, full of souvenirs from all the exciting times they'd shared together.

"That vacation on Rainspell Island was really special," Rachel said, pointing at the ferry tickets and map that had been stuck into the book.

"I know," Kirsty replied, smiling. "It was the first time we met each other — and the first time we met the fairies, too!" She lowered her voice. "I wonder if we'll have a fairy adventure this week."

"I hope so," Rachel said, feeling her heart thump excitedly at the thought. She and her parents were spending her school vacation with Kirsty's family, and she had been wondering the same thing herself. Somehow, extra-special things always seemed to happen when she and Kirsty got together!

The girls kept looking through their book. There was the museum pamphlet from the day they'd met Storm the Lightning Fairy; tickets to Strawberry

Farms, where they'd helped Georgia the Guinea Pig Fairy; plus all sorts of photos, postcards, maps, petals, and leaves. . . .

Kirsty frowned when she spotted an empty space on one page. "Did a picture fall out?" she wondered.

"It must have," Rachel said. "You can see that something was stuck there before. I think it was a picture of the fairy models we painted the day we met Willow the Wednesday Fairy. I wonder where it went."

As the girls turned more pages, they realized that photo wasn't the only thing missing. A map of the constellations that Kirsty's gran had given them the night they'd helped Stephanie the Starfish Fairy had vanished, and so had the all-access pass they'd had for the Fairyland Games. Each time they turned a page, they discovered something even worse.

"Oh, no! This photo of us at Camp Stargaze is torn," Rachel said in dismay.

"This page has scribbles all over it," Kirsty cried. "How did that happen?"

"And where did *this* picture come from?" Rachel asked, pointing at a colorful image of a pretty little fairy. She had shoulder-length blond hair that was pinned back with a pink star-shaped clip. She wore a sparkly lilac top and a ruffled blue skirt with a colorful belt, and pink sparkly ankle boots. "I've never even seen her before!" She bit her lip. "Something weird is going on, Kirsty. You don't think —"

Before Rachel could finish her sentence,

the picture of the fairy began to sparkle and glitter with all the colors of the rainbow. The girls watched, wide-eyed, as the fairy fluttered her wings, stretched, and then flew right off the page in a whirl of twinkling dust!

"Oh!" Kirsty gasped. "Hello! What's your name? How did you get into our memory book?"

The fairy smiled, shook out her wings, and flew a loop-the-loop. "I'm Florence the Friendship Fairy," she said in a sweet voice, her bright eyes darting around the room. "You're Kirsty and Rachel, aren't you? I've heard so much about you! I know you've been good friends to the fairies many, many times before."

"It's so nice to meet you," Rachel said. "But, Florence, do you know what happened to our memory book? Things are missing from the pages, and some things have even been ruined."

Florence fluttered over and landed on the bed. "I'm afraid that's the reason I came here," she said sadly. "Special memory books, scrapbooks, and photo albums everywhere have been ruined and stolen — so I need your help!"

RAINBOW magic

These activities are magical!
Play dress-up, send friendship notes, and much more!

SCHOLASTIC
www.scholastic.com
www.rainbowmagiconline.com

HiT entertainment

RMACTIV3

RAINBOW magic™

There's Magic in Every Series!

The Rainbow Fairies
The Weather Fairies
The Jewel Fairies
The Pet Fairies
The Fun Day Fairies
The Petal Fairies
The Dance Fairies
The Music Fairies
The Sports Fairies
The Party Fairies
The Ocean Fairies
The Night Fairies
The Magical Animal Fairies
The Princess Fairies

Read them all!

■ SCHOLASTIC

www.scholastic.com
www.rainbowmagiconline.com

HiT entertainment

RMFAIRY6